my first 100 NUMBERS

1

one teddy bear

2

two cherries

3

three dolls

4

four fishes

5

five animals

6

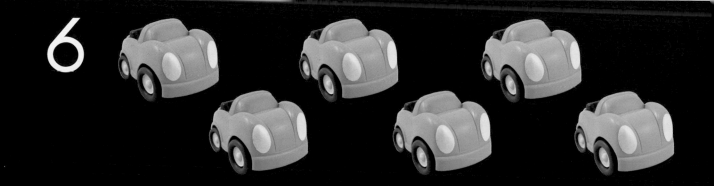

7

seven balls

8

eight forks

9

nine bows

10

ten easter eggs

11

eleven stars

12

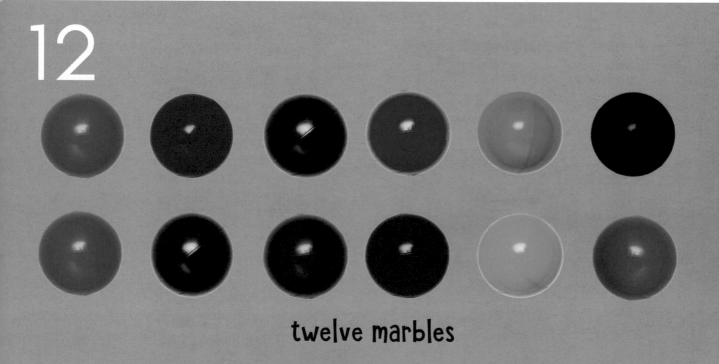

twelve marbles

13

thirteen dump trucks

14

15

fifteen donuts

16

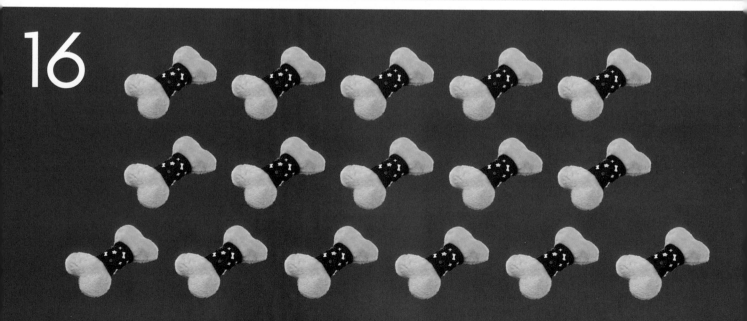

sixteen chew toys

17

seventeen gifts

18

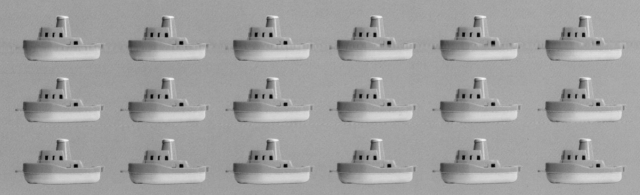

eighteen toy ships

19

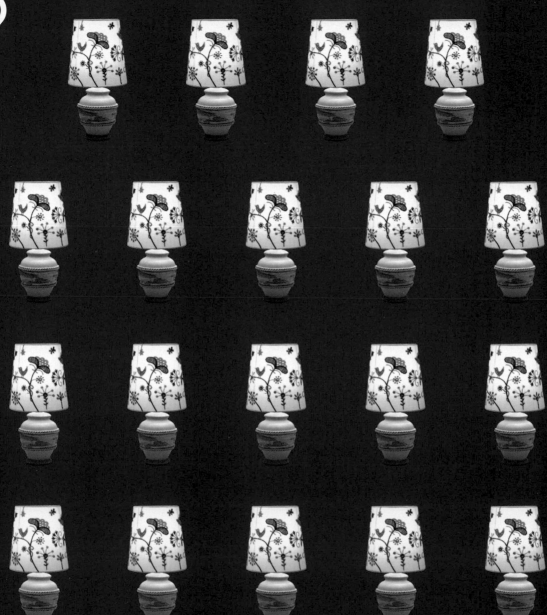

nineteen table lamps

20

twenty toy giraffes

let's count up to 100

41 42 43 44 45

46 47 48 49 50

51 52 53 54 55

56 57 58 59 60

61 62 63 64 65

66 67 68 69 70

71 72 73 74 75

76 77 78 79 80

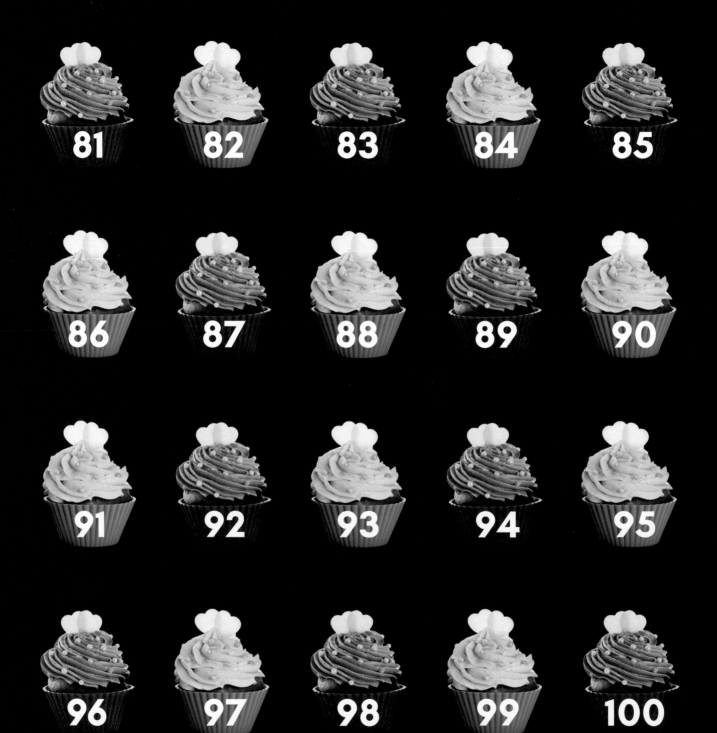